MY FIRST

I Can Read

LOOSE TOOTH

story by **Lola M. Schaefer**
pictures by **Sylvie Wickstrom**

SCHOLASTIC INC.

New York Toronto London Auckland Sydney
Mexico City New Delhi Hong Kong Buenos Aires

ISBN-13: 978-0-439-89902-4
ISBN-10: 0-439-89902-8

Text copyright © 2004 by Lola M. Schaefer.
Illustrations copyright © 2004 by Sylvie Wickstrom. All rights reserved.
Published by Scholastic Inc., 557 Broadway, New York, NY 10012,
by arrangement with HarperCollins Publishers.
SCHOLASTIC and associated logos are trademarks
and/or registered trademarks of Scholastic Inc.

12 11 10 9 8 7 6 5 4 3 2 1   6 7 8 9 10 11/0

Printed in the U.S.A.   23

First Scholastic printing, September 2006

I Can Read Book® is a trademark of HarperCollins Publishers Inc.

For Maddie
—L.S.

To Sosha,
who just lost another tooth
—S.W.

It's loose.

It's loose.

My tooth is loose!

I can see it.

I can feel it.

I can pull it.

I can push it.

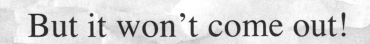

But it won't come out!

It's loose.

It's loose.

My tooth is loose!

I wiggled it for Brother.

I wiggled it for Mom.

I wiggled it for Sister,

and my good friend Tom.

But it won't come out!

It's loose.

It's loose.

My tooth is loose!

I just ate an apple.

I bit a hard nut.

I chewed a long carrot.

And—guess what?

My tooth is loose,

loose,

loose.

But it won't come out!

Brother says, "Pull it!"

Sister says, "Wait."

Dad says, "Let's see."

Mom says, "Too late!"

My tooth came out

with NO help from me.

Now there's a hole
where my tooth
used to be!